Dirty Bertie

MUD!

For Kate, James and little 'O' ~ D R
For everyone at Greythorn
Primary School ~ A M

STRIPES PUBLISHING
An imprint of Magi Publications
1 The Coda Centre, 189 Munster Road,
London SW6 6AW

A paperback original
First published in Great Britain in 2009

Characters created by David Roberts
Text copyright © Alan MacDonald, 2009
Illustrations copyright © David Roberts, 2009

ISBN: 978-1-84715-072-1

Printed and bound in Belgium.

10 9 8 7 6 5 4 3 2 1

Dirty Bertie

MUD!

DAVID ROBERTS WRITTEN BY ALAN MACDONALD

stripes

Collect all the
Dirty Bertie books!

Coming soon:

Contents

MUD!

CHAPTER 1

"BERTIE! HANDS OUT OF YOUR POCKETS!" thundered Miss Boot.

"I'm cold, Miss," moaned Bertie.

"Then run around!"

Bertie made a feeble show of stamping his feet. He hated football practice. Why did Miss Boot have to drag them outside in the freezing cold?

Dirty Bertie

Why couldn't they practise indoors?

Bertie was brilliant at watching football. He was terrific at talking about it. He just wasn't any good at *playing it*. During a game he never seemed to be in the right place. Most of the time he watched the ball zooming back and forward over his head. And when it did come his way everyone yelled advice: "PASS! MOVE IT! CROSS IT!" Bertie dithered – and by the time he made up his mind, the ball was at the other end of the pitch.

Miss Boot started the lesson with some warm-up exercises. She was wearing her bright orange tracksuit, the one which made her look like a giant satsuma. The class dribbled in and out of cones. They passed back and forth. They practised heading the ball without squealing.

After ten minutes, Miss Boot called them together.

"Before we start a game, I have some good news. From this term the Pudsley Junior team has a new coach. Me."

"Hooray!" cheered Know-All Nick.

A lump of mud hit him on the ear. Bertie looked up at the sky and whistled.

Dirty Bertie

"Now, we have an important match on Friday and I am looking for new players," Miss Boot went on. "Who would like to play for the school team?"

A dozen hands shot up. Bertie kept his hands by his sides. He shivered. He tried pulling his shirt down over his knees to keep warm.

"Excellent," said Miss Boot. "And hands up if you want to play in goal?"

No hands went up.

Bertie felt someone pinch his arm.

"YOW!" he cried.

Know-All Nick looked up at the sky.

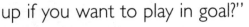

"Bertie!" said Miss Boot. "Are you volunteering?"

"Me?" said Bertie.

"Yes, have you played in goal before?"

"No, no … I can't… I don't…"

"He's just being modest, Miss!" said Nick, thumping Bertie on the back. "Ask anyone, he's brilliant!"

"Hmm," said Miss Boot. Brilliant was not a word she connected with Bertie. Surely there had to be someone else?

"What about you, Nicholas?" she said.

"I can't, Miss. I've got weak ankles," simpered Nick.

"Really," said Miss Boot. "Eugene, how about you?"

"Sorry, my mum doesn't like me playing football."

"Trevor?"

Dirty Bertie

"Haven't got any boots, Miss."

Bertie looked around in desperation.
Surely *someone* wanted to play in goal?

"That settles it then," sighed Miss Boot.
"You are in goal on Friday, Bertie. *DO
NOT LET ME DOWN.*"

"But Miss—" began Bertie.

Miss Boot blew a shrill blast on her
whistle and bustled off to
start the game.

Dirty Bertie

Bertie stared after her. This couldn't be happening. Him playing in goal for the school team? It was a disaster! A nightmare! Bertie had never played in goal in his life, not even in the playground. He didn't know how to save a ball – he couldn't even save his pocket money. That two-faced toad Nick was behind this. He knew very well Bertie was no good at football. He just wanted to see him make a fool of himself.

After the practice, Bertie trudged back to school with Darren, Eugene and Donna.

"Never mind," said Donna. "It wasn't that bad."

"No," said Darren. "When you kept your eyes open you did much better."

Dirty Bertie

Know-All Nick caught up with them.
His shirt and shorts were spotless.

"Hey, Bertie, what was the score
again? Remind me," he smirked.

Bertie ignored him.

"Six? Or was it seven? I lost count."

"At least Miss Boot won't want me in
the team," said Bertie.

Dirty Bertie

"That's where you're wrong," grinned Nick. "There's no one else."

Bertie groaned. "Why me? Can't someone else go in goal?"

"No thanks!" said Darren. "I'm a striker. Anyway, goalies always get the blame when you lose."

"You think we'll lose?" asked Bertie.

"Are you kidding?" said Darren. "We're playing Cropper Lane."

Bertie looked blank.

"They're top of the league," said Donna. "They haven't lost a match."

"HA! HA!" gurgled Nick. "It'll be a thrashing! I'm *definitely* coming to watch. I wouldn't miss this for anything!"

CHAPTER 2

Bertie plodded home after school. Over supper he broke the news to his parents.

"The school team?" said Dad. "That's terrific!"

"Mmm," said Bertie. "Except they want me to play in goal."

"Well that's good, isn't it?" beamed Mum. "You don't look very excited."

"Of course he's excited," said Dad.
"I had no idea you played in goal, Bertie."

"I don't!" groaned Bertie. "That's the
point. I only got picked by mistake!"

"Don't be silly," said Mum. "You're
probably better than you think."

"I'M NOT!" wailed Bertie. "I'm rubbish!"

"Well I'm sure it'll be fine," said Mum.
"As long as you do your best no one's
going to mind."

Bertie thought Miss Boot would mind.
Miss Boot hated losing at anything –
even tiddlywinks. If Bertie played badly
she'd probably use him as a football and
boot him round the pitch.

Dad had fetched his old trainers
from the hall. "I used to play football
a bit myself," he said. "Just over in the
park, but I was pretty good."

Dirty Bertie

"Really?" said Bertie. It was the first he'd heard about it.

"Why don't we have a kick-about in the garden? I could give you a few tips."

Five minutes later, Bertie stood between two flower-pot goalposts. He was wearing his woolly gloves and a baseball cap. Dad bounced the ball a few times and placed it on the lawn.

"Now," he said, "make yourself big. Not like that, crouch down. Arms wide, head up, eye on the ball. Now I'm going to come at you, try to put me off."

Bertie waved his arms. "MISS, MISS, MISS!" he yelled.

"What are you doing?" asked Dad.

"Putting you off."

"Not like that. I mean come out!"

"I thought I was in goal!" said Bertie.

Dirty Bertie

Dad sighed. "Listen. I'll take a shot, you just try and stop it, OK?"

Dad took three steps back. He ran up and thumped the ball with all his might. Bertie watched it sail miles over his head into next-door's garden.

CRASH! TINKLE!

"Whoops," said Dad. "Maybe we'll finish this another time."

Dirty Bertie

The next few days passed in a daze. Bertie couldn't get the football match out of his mind. Even in his sleep he had nightmares about it. He dreamed he was playing against a team of Miss Boots. Miss Boot dribbled. She passed to Miss Boot. Miss Boot shot. Bertie dived…

He woke up on his bedroom floor, cold with sweat.

CHAPTER 3

The day of the big match arrived.
Bertie stared at the drops of rain
running down the minibus window.
He was doomed.

"Cheer up," said Darren. "What's the
worst that can happen?"

"We lose," said Bertie. "And I let in
twenty goals."

"You won't!" said Darren. "You're not *that* bad."

"No?" said Bertie.

"No!" said Darren. "You're just not very good."

"Thanks," said Bertie. Donna turned round from the seat in front.

"You never know, you might play well," she said. "We might even win."

"Against Cropper Lane?" said Darren.

"Hey, Bertie!" called a loud voice behind them. "Catch!"

Bertie turned round. A toffee hit him on the nose.

"HA! HA!" jeered Know-All Nick. "Call yourself a goalie? You can't catch for toffee!"

Dirty Bertie

The rain fell in buckets as the bus turned
into the school drive and came to a halt.
The Pudsley Junior team trooped off.
They stared at the field. It sloped like the
deck of a sinking ship. There were a few
tufts of grass – the rest
was a sea of mud.
A seagull swam
in one of the
puddles.
   Bertie felt a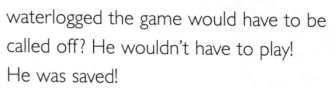
wave of relief.
Surely if the
pitch was
waterlogged the game would have to be
called off? He wouldn't have to play!
He was saved!
   "Right, hurry up and get changed,"
barked Miss Boot, putting up her umbrella.

"But Miss, what about the pitch?"
said Bertie.

"What about it?"

"It's a bog. We can't play on that!"

"Nonsense! A few little puddles never
hurt anyone. In my day we played
hockey when the snow was up to our
knees!"

Just then the Cropper Lane team ran
out in their red shirts. They warmed up,
taking it in turns to blast the ball into
one of the goals.

Know-All Nick sidled over. "Pretty big
aren't they? Look at that number nine.
I wouldn't want to get in *his* way."
He gave Bertie a sickly smile.

Bertie stomped off to the dressing
room to get changed.

CHAPTER 4

SPLODGE, SPLODGE, SPLODGE.

Bertie paddled around in his goalmouth.
So far he hadn't let in any goals.
Considering they'd been playing for five
minutes this was pretty good. He was
already rather dirty but that didn't bother
him. Bertie loved mud. Adults were
always shouting at him to keep out of it.

25

But goalkeepers were actually *expected* to get muddy. It was part of the job.

Bertie sploshed through a puddle. *I wonder what it's like for mud sliding?* he thought. Taking a run, he skidded across his goal. Mud sprayed everywhere. Not bad. Next he chose the biggest puddle in the goal. This time he skidded right through it.

THUMP! WHOOSH!

Something zoomed past his head. He looked up. Why was everyone cheering? The Cropper Lane players were all crowding round the number nine. Bertie turned his head slowly. A football nestled in the back of the net.

Miss Boot turned crimson.

"BERTIE!" she thundered. "WHAT ARE YOU PLAYING AT?"

Dirty Bertie

"Sorry! I wasn't watching," said Bertie.

Darren picked the ball out of the net.

"You're meant to try and stop it,"
he grumbled.

"I wasn't ready!" complained Bertie.
"Somebody should tell me if they're going
to shoot!"

Pudsley Juniors kicked off. Bertie
sighed. This was exactly why he hadn't
wanted to play in goal. You stood around
for ages freezing to death then everyone
blamed you for one tiny mistake.

From the touchline
Know-All Nick
gave him a
thumbs-up
sign.

"Nice one,
Bertie!" he jeered.

Dirty Bertie

For the rest of the half, Bertie tried to
focus on the game. It wasn't too hard as
most of the action took place around his
goal. Cropper Lane were well on top.
Pudsley got everyone back and defended
grimly. Bertie dived, slipped and sloshed
in the mud as shots rained in like
hailstones. One crashed off the post.
Another thudded off the
crossbar. A third squirted
through Bertie's legs and was
going in until it got stuck
in a puddle.

Dirty Bertie

At half-time the Pudsley players
trudged off, grateful to be only one
goal down. Their coach was not pleased.

"USELESS! PATHETIC!" screeched
Miss Boot. "I didn't come all this way to
see you lose! Now go out there and
get back in this game!"

The second half began. The rain fell in
sheets. Bertie got muddier and muddier.
His shirt stuck to his back. His shorts
were brown. His boots sucked and

squelched every time he moved.

Then the miracle happened. Pudsley scored! It was Donna who surprised everyone, ending a mazy dribble by poking the ball home.

"GOAL!" bellowed Miss Boot, waving her umbrella.

"GOAL!" cried Bertie, doing a handstand in the mud.

Know-All Nick shook his head. The Cropper Lane players looked at each other in disbelief. With five minutes left, the scores were level at 1-1.

"Come on, Pudsley!" roared Miss Boot. "You can do it!"

Cropper Lane kicked off. Pudsley cleared the ball, booting it anywhere. From a throw-in the number nine barged his way into the penalty area.

Dirty Bertie

"Come out, Bertie!" yelled Darren.
Bertie tore out of his goal like an
express train. He skidded in the mud
and couldn't stop… "ARGH!" cried the
number nine as Bertie flattened him.

"PEEP!" The referee pointed to the
spot for a penalty.

The Pudsley players groaned. Only a
few minutes left and Bertie was going to
cost them the game.

Dirty Bertie

Bertie picked himself up and splodged back to his goal line. *Typical*, he thought, *now we're going to lose and everyone will blame me.*

He crouched with his hands at the ready. He'd never faced a penalty before.

The number nine pawed the ground. He began his run-up. Bertie heard someone singing loudly behind his goal:

"There's only one Pudsley goalie,

Dirty Bertie

And his pants are all holey…!"

Bertie swung round to see Know-All
Nick's grinning face.

THUD! … WHACK!

Something thumped him on the back
of the head, sending him sprawling. Half-
dazed, Bertie saw a ball bounce in the
mud. He reached out to grab it before it
could cross the line. Seconds later he
was mobbed by his teammates.

Dirty Bertie

"Brilliant, Bertie!"

"What a save!"

"You weren't even looking!"

They crowded round him, slapping him on the back. Bertie grinned and spat out a piece of grass.

Soon after, the whistle blew for the end of the game. The Pudsley players threw their arms in the air. Miss Boot danced in the puddles. A draw against the might of Cropper Lane was as good as a victory. Bertie was carried off the pitch by his cheering teammates. He caught sight of a scowling boy trying to slink away unseen. Bertie scooped a clod of mud off his shirt and took aim…

SPLAT!

CHEESE!

CHAPTER 1

It was twenty to nine. Bertie was late for school.

"Bertie! Hurry up!" yelled his mum.

"I'm not going!"

"Get down here now!" cried Mum. "I'm counting to five."

"The door's stuck! I can't get out!"

Mum folded her arms. "One, two,

three, four … four and a half…"

The bathroom door burst open and
Bertie stomped downstairs.

"At last," said Mum. "Let's have a look at
you. There, I think you look very smart."

Bertie stared at his reflection in the
hall mirror. He hardly recognized himself.
He was wearing a clean white shirt and
school tie. His face glowed a healthy
pink. His hair had been washed for the
first time in months. Instead of
resembling a bird's
nest, it was neatly
combed and
parted.

"I look
ridiculous," moaned
Bertie. "Why can't
I dress normally?"

"You know why," replied Mum. "It's the class photo today and I want you to look your best."

Bertie tugged at his tie.

"It's strangling me! I can't breathe!"

"Well you'll have to put up with it," said Mum. "Just for once, I'd like a class photo I can keep."

"But we've got millions of photos of me!" said Bertie.

"Yes and you're pulling a face in all of them."

Bertie sighed. It wasn't his fault his class photos were never any good. Photographers always made the class stand around for ages. It was boring. By the time they did take the photo Bertie had lost interest and was looking the wrong way.

Dirty Bertie

Mr Weakly's class
Pudsley Juniors

Mum straightened his tie. "Anyway, this year you're going to be smart. And I expect you to stay like this all day."

"OK, I'll try," groaned Bertie, wiping his nose on his hand.

Mum sighed wearily. Bertie had trouble staying clean for five minutes, let alone a whole day.

"Tell you what," she said, "I'll make you a deal. If you bring home a nice class photo I'll take you to that water park."

"Splash City?" gasped Bertie.

Splash City had just opened in town and all Bertie's friends had been. It had a giant bubble pool, six flumes and the Rocky Rapids River Ride. Bertie was willing to do anything for a trip to Splash City – even stay clean for a day.

"Is it a deal?" said Mum.

"Deal," said Bertie, excitedly.

"Good. Have you got your hanky?"

Bertie pulled it out of his pocket.

"Remember to use it before the photo," said Mum. "I don't want a picture of you with a runny nose."

"OK!" sighed Bertie.

Dirty Bertie

"And don't lose it. No hanky, no trip
to Splash City – understand?"

Bertie tucked his hanky up his sleeve
and hurried off down the road. He
couldn't wait for the weekend. All he had
to do was stay clean for one day – how
hard could it be?

CHAPTER 2

Bertie stood in the playground with his friends, waiting for the bell.

"What's that funny smell?" asked Darren, holding his nose.

"It's Bertie," grinned Eugene. "He's had a bath!"

Darren sniffed Bertie. "Phew! You smell of flowers!"

"It's just shampoo!" said Bertie.

"And what's wrong with your hair?" said Eugene.

Bertie rolled his eyes. "My mum did it. It's for the photo."

"I think you look sweet," giggled Donna.

"SWEET?" hooted Darren. "He looks like an alien! Anyway, I bet you can't stay like that for five minutes."

"That's where you're wrong," said Bertie. "'Cos if I stay clean my mum's taking me to Splash City."

Just then a pale boy arrived carrying a briefcase. It was Bertie's arch-enemy, Know-All Nick. Nick halted and stared at Bertie. Bertie stared back. They looked like twins.

"What happened to you?" sneered Nick.

"Nothing," said Bertie.

"You look weird. Have you brushed your hair?" Bertie sighed.

"If you must know it's for the photo. I thought I'd look smart."

"You? Smart? HA! HA!" scoffed Nick.

Bertie glanced down. Nick was standing close to a large brown puddle. If he jumped in it now he could splash Nick with muddy water. But he was bound to get dirty as well — and he'd promised his mum to stay clean. Still, there was always tomorrow.

He turned to go. "See you later, smarty-pants."

Dirty Bertie

Miss Boot prowled the front of the classroom.

"I trust you've all remembered that we're having our class photo today," she said. "And this year I don't want anyone spoiling it – Bertie."

"Me?" said Bertie.

"Yes, you," glared Miss Boot. "Don't think I've forgotten last year."

"That wasn't my dog!" said Bertie. "He followed me into school…"

"Quiet!" barked Miss Boot. "This year there will be no dogs and no silliness, do I make myself clear?"

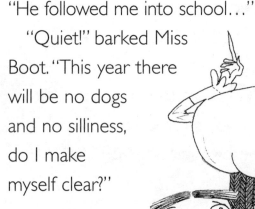

Dirty Bertie

"Yes, Miss Boot," chorused the class.

"Good. The photographer is arriving at one o'clock, so we will gather in the hall after lunch."

Bertie groaned. After lunch? That meant he had to get through an entire morning without getting dirty. Still, it would be worth it. Bertie sniffed.
He was about to wipe his nose on his sleeve when he remembered his hanky. He reached into his trouser pocket.
He turned cold. It wasn't there!
He checked his other pocket.

Empty!

What was it his mum had said? *No hanky, no trip to Splash City.* Bertie slumped forward on his desk. This was terrible – if he didn't find it, there'd be no Rocky Rapids River Ride.

Dirty Bertie

Miss Boot was busy writing sums on the board. Slowly, Bertie slid down in his seat and disappeared under his desk. His eyes swept across the floor. No sign of a hanky. He began to crawl on all fours, weaving his way through a forest of legs. The floor was littered with sweet wrappers, stickers, chewing gum, rubbers, apple cores and dead bluebottles – but no hanky.

"OW!"

Uh oh – he'd accidentally crawled over someone's foot.

"Nicholas!" cried Miss Boot. "Get on with your work!"

"It wasn't me, Miss," whined Know-All Nick. "Someone kicked me!"

"Don't talk nonsense!" snapped Miss Boot.

Dirty Bertie

Bertie kept very still. Suddenly Nick's head appeared under the desk and their eyes met. Bertie put a finger to his lips and shook his head. A sly smile spread across Nick's face.

"It's Bertie, Miss!" cried Nick. "He's under the table!"

Bertie groaned. Trust Know-All to tell tales.

"BERTIE!" thundered Miss Boot. "COME OUT FROM THERE, THIS MINUTE!"

Slowly Bertie crawled out and stood up. His trousers seemed to have got rather dusty. A lump of chewing gum was stuck to his knee.

"Well? What do you have to say for yourself?" demanded Miss Boot.

"Um ... have you seen my hanky?" asked Bertie.

CHAPTER 3

Miss Boot kept Bertie in at morning break, which meant he had no chance to look for his missing hanky. By lunchtime he was beginning to panic. Time was running out. Maybe he'd dropped the hanky in the playground when he got to school?

Mr Grouch was over by the railings,

sweeping up litter. Normally Bertie
did his best to avoid the caretaker.
Mr Grouch didn't like children and he
especially didn't like Bertie. Bertie was
pretty sure that he turned into a
vampire after dark. Nevertheless this
was an emergency.

"Um … Mr Grouch?"

The caretaker
carried on sweeping.

"I was wondering if you'd seen a hanky? It's sort of white…"

Mr Grouch scowled. "I know what a hanky looks like."

"Oh. Have you seen it?"

"Do I look like I'm running a lost property service?"

"No, but…"

Mr Grouch leaned heavily on his broom.

"Anything I find in this playground is treated as litter," he said. "Litter goes in the bin, got that?"

"Yes … er, thanks," said Bertie, beating a hasty retreat.

Bertie hurried round the side of the school. He found two large, grey bins standing in a corner. They were taller than he was. Even standing on tiptoe he couldn't see inside.

Dirty Bertie

Luckily help was at hand.

"Hi, Bertie. What are you doing?" asked Eugene, appearing at his side.

"Quick," said Bertie. "Get down."

"What?"

"I need to climb on your back!"

"But it's dirty!" grumbled Eugene. "I'm wearing my best clothes."

"This is an emergency," said Bertie. "I've got to find my hanky."

"What if Mr Grouch catches us?"

"He won't. Come on!"

Eugene sighed and got down on all fours. Bertie climbed on to his back. He lifted the lid of the first bin and peeped inside. It was full of leftovers from dinner. It smelled worse than one of Darren's burps.

"Can you see it?" asked Eugene.

"I'm looking. Keep still!" said Bertie.

"Hurry up, I can't hold you!"

Eugene was getting anxious. He thought he could hear footsteps. Someone was coming and he was sure it was Mr Grouch! He leaped to his feet.

"WOOOAHHHHH!" cried Bertie, losing his balance. He grabbed hold of the bin. It toppled towards him.

CRAAAASH!

Bertie surfaced from under a mountain of rotten cabbage and potato peel.

"S-sorry, Bertie!" stammered Eugene.

Bertie shook his head, scattering bits of vegetable in all directions.

"HEY YOU! COME HERE!" yelled an angry voice.

Mr Grouch was striding towards them waving his broom like a Roman spear.

Dirty Bertie

Bertie didn't wait around to explain.
He ran for his life.

Bertie ducked into the cloakroom to
give Mr Grouch the slip. There were only
five minutes till the end of lunch break
and he still hadn't found his hanky.

Dirty Bertie

"Phoo! What happened to you?"
asked Know-All Nick, poking his head
round the door. Bertie looked up.
A white triangle peeped from Nick's
top pocket. A hanky!

"Where did you get that?"

"This? It's mine," said Nick.

"Liar! You stole it! It's mine."

Bertie made a grab for it, but Nick
dodged aside and waved the hanky
under his
nose.

"See, it's
got the
letter 'N' for
Nicholas.
I expect

yours has a 'B' for Bogeynose."

Bertie glared at him.

"What's the matter?" taunted Nick. "Did poor lickle Bertie lose his hanky?"

"Get lost," Bertie snapped.

"Please yourself," shrugged Nick. "I was going to tell you where to find it, but maybe I won't."

"You've seen it?" said Bertie. "Where?"

Nick smiled slyly. "In the boys' toilets. But you'll have to hurry."

Bertie flew down the corridor. He raced past the classrooms, screeched round a corner and crashed through the door of the boys' toilets.

SPLOOSH! His feet went from under him and he sat down with a bump.

He looked around. The floor was ankle deep in water and his trousers were soaking wet. It was then that he noticed the sign on the door.

KEEP OUT

TOILETS FLOODED!
NO ENTRY!
THAT MEANS YOU!

By Order G. R. Grouch

Bertie got soggily to his feet. That two-faced sneak had tricked him. There was no hanky. And now he was dripping wet *and* late for the class photo.

CHAPTER 4

Miss Boot arranged her class on the platform in the hall. At last everyone was in position. She counted the heads and groaned. Someone was missing and no prizes for guessing who.

Right on cue the door flew open and Bertie rushed in, panting for breath.

Miss Boot stared at him in horror.

Dirty Bertie

"Good grief! What on earth have you been doing?"

"Me? Nothing," said Bertie.

"Look at the state of you!" said Miss Boot, clutching her head.

Bertie inspected himself. Come to think of it, he was a little messy. His trousers were caked in dust and dripping wet. His clean white shirt was stained a greenish brown. A wet puddle was spreading around his feet. He pushed back his hair and a piece of potato peel fell out.

Dirty Bertie

"Go and get cleaned up," ordered Miss Boot. "No wait, there isn't time. Stand in the back row and try to keep out of sight."

Bertie splodged on to the platform and pushed his way to the back next to Darren.

The photographer bent over his camera.

"Everyone ready? Say cheese!"

"Cheese!" chorused the class.

"WAIT!" cried a voice.

Miss Boot groaned. "What is it *now*, Bertie?"

"I need to blow my nose."

"Then blow it. And use a hanky."

"That's the trouble," wailed Bertie. "I've been looking everywhere and I can't find it!"

"Then you'll *have to do without!*"
screeched Miss Boot. "Now can we
please get on with the photo?"

The photographer bent over his
camera once more. Bertie's shoulders
drooped. His nose was running but
what did it matter? Once his mum
discovered he'd lost his hanky there'd
be no trip to Splash City.

He found a dry patch on his sleeve
and wiped his nose. Wait a minute …
what was that? A corner of white
peeped out from under his cuff. And
then he remembered. He'd stuffed his
hanky into his sleeve that morning for
safe keeping. He pulled it out
triumphantly. Everything was going to
be OK. He put the hanky to his nose
and blew…

Dirty Bertie

CLICK!

Miss Boot's class

Pudsley Juniors

Dirty Bertie

Mum was busy on the computer when she heard the front door open.

"Bertie, is that you? How did the photo go?"

"Fine," shouted Bertie, coming into the room.

Mum turned round. She turned pale. She looked like she might faint.

"Bertie…! WHAT HAVE YOU DONE?!" she gasped.

"It's OK!" beamed Bertie. "I lost my hanky but I found it. Look!"

He waved a soggy white rag.

"So," he said, "can we go?"

Mum stared. "Go? Go where?"

"To Splash City. You promised!"

Mum looked grim. "There's only one

Dirty Bertie

place you're going, Bertie, and there
won't be any splashing."

SPOOKY!

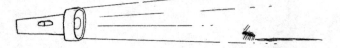

CHAPTER 1

Bertie couldn't wait – Darren and
Eugene were coming for a sleepover and
they were going to sleep in the tent in
the garden. All he had to do was
convince his parents.

"I'm sorry, Bertie," said Mum, "I don't
think it's a good idea."

"Why not?" asked Bertie.

"Because last time you woke up all the neighbours!"

"We were only having a water fight."

"It was two in the morning! We had half the street banging on the door."

"We won't do it again," promised Bertie. "We'll be really, really quiet."

Mum sighed wearily. "In any case, I don't even know where the tent is."

Dad came into the kitchen.

"Dad," said Bertie, "do you know where the tent is?"

"Mmm? In the garage I expect."

"Can we sleep in it tonight?"

"I don't see why not."

"Great!" said Bertie.

The doorbell rang and he dashed off to answer it before his parents could change their minds.

"Guess what?" said Bertie, as Darren
and Eugene staggered through the front
door carrying their bags. "Mum and Dad
said yes. We can sleep in the tent!"

"Brilliant!" said Darren. "We can have
a water fight!"

They found the tent under a pile of
junk at the back of the garage. It had
been Dad's brilliant idea to buy it.

He said they'd have lots of wonderful family camping holidays and save a fortune. But as it turned out they'd only been camping once. It had rained all weekend, the tent nearly blew away in a gale and their sleeping bags had got soaked. They'd left in the morning with Mum vowing she would never go camping again.

Bertie shook out the contents of the bag on to the grass. Eugene stared at the jumble of pegs and poles.

"Shouldn't we read the instructions?" he asked.

"No need," said Bertie. "It's simple! I've done it hundreds of times!"

This wasn't strictly true – the tent had only been up twice and Bertie hadn't helped at all.

Dirty Bertie

Bertie and Eugene wrestled with the
poles while Whiffer got in the way and
sat on the groundsheet. Darren lolled on
the grass reading a comic.
At last they were finished
and Bertie stood back
to admire their work.

Dirty Bertie

"It looks a bit wonky," frowned Darren.

"It's meant to be wonky," said Bertie.

"Can I let go of the pole now?" called Eugene from inside.

"Wait a minute!" answered Bertie. "I've got to do the pegs."

Bertie went round with a mallet hammering pegs into the ground. Darren went back to his comic. Whiffer was sniffing round the tent, eager to join in. He seized one of the guy ropes in his mouth and started to pull. The peg shot out. The tent leaned dangerously to one side.

"NO!" yelled Bertie. "Whiffer, let go!"

"GRRRR!" growled Whiffer, shaking his head from side to side.

"Bad dog!" cried Bertie, trying to grab the rope.

Dirty Bertie

Whiffer backed away, the rope still in his teeth. The tent stretched. *And stretched.*

TWANG! A dozen pegs shot out of the ground and the tent collapsed in a heap.

"MNNNNFF HEEELP!" cried a voice from underneath.

"OK, Eugene, you can let go now," said Bertie.

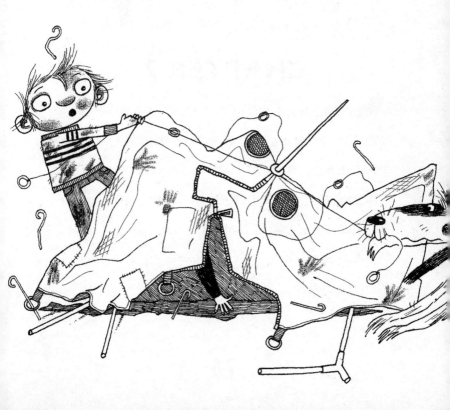

CHAPTER 2

After supper, Dad went out to the garden to sort out the tent. Bertie sat in his bedroom with Darren and Eugene checking their supplies for the night.

"Comics?" said Bertie.

"Check."

"Torches?"

"Check."

Dirty Bertie

"Midnight feast?"

"I brought the crisps," said Darren.

"I got the chocolate biscuits," said Bertie.

"I got some muesli bars," said Eugene.

The other two gave him a look.

"What? It's all I could get! My mum says they're good for you."

Bertie rolled his eyes. "What about weapons? Is everybody armed?"

Darren had a space gun he'd got for his birthday. Bertie tucked his pirate dagger into his belt. Only Eugene had forgotten.

"Why do we need weapons, anyway?" he asked.

Bertie shrugged. "Don't say we didn't warn you."

"It'll be dark," said Darren. "Really dark. You never know what might be *out there*."

Eugene turned pale. "You're just trying to scare me," he said.

Mum poked her head round the door.

"OK, the tent's all ready!"

"Great," said Bertie.

"Wicked!" said Darren.

"Hooray," gulped Eugene, gripping his torch.

Tiptoe, tiptoe, tiptoe. The three of them crept down the garden.

Bertie led the way with Eugene keeping close behind. In the dark the garden seemed much bigger than Bertie remembered. The moon was a ghostly white. The trees threw dancing shadows on the ground.

"Wait!" said Bertie, halting suddenly. "Where's Darren?"

They looked around. "He was here a minute ago," said Eugene.

They shone their torches into the bushes.

"Darren?" called Bertie. "Where are you?"

No answer. The tent flapped in the wind.

"Darren, this isn't funny. Come out!"

Dirty Bertie

Silence.

"Maybe he went back for something?" whispered Eugene.

They looked back at the house. Whiffer watched them hopefully from the kitchen where he was locked in for the night.

There was a rustle in the bushes. Bertie swung round.

"Darren? Is that you?"

Deathly silence.

"Maybe we better wait in the tent," said Bertie.

"G-good idea," stammered Eugene.

They both bolted down the garden. Eugene wrestled with the zip…

"GRARRRRRRGH!"

Something burst out of the bushes and grabbed Bertie round the neck.

"YEEAARGH! HEEELP!" howled Bertie.

Dirty Bertie

"HA! HA! HA!" giggled Darren. "Did
I scare you?"

Bertie struggled free. "Course not."

"Liar! You practically wet your pants."

"Didn't."

"Did."

Dirty Bertie

"Didn't. We knew it was you, didn't we, Eugene? *Eugene?*"

Eugene peeped his head out of the tent. "Has it gone?"

Darren was still going on about his clever trick as they got into their sleeping bags. *Right that's it*, thought Bertie. *Two can play at that game.* No one made a fool of Bertie, the terror of Class 3. Who had locked Mr Weakly in the cupboard? Who had turned the hose on Mr Grouch, the demon caretaker? *We'll soon find out which of us is the scaredy-cat*, scowled Bertie. By the time he had finished Darren would be begging for his mum.

CHAPTER 3

"Pass the crisps," said Bertie.

"All gone," said Darren.

"Throw me a biscuit, then."

"None left."

"There's still some muesli bars," said Eugene.

Bertie burped. Wrappers, crisp packets and biscuit crumbs littered the tent.

He brushed them off his sleeping bag. They'd read their comics, made shadows with their torches and eaten their midnight feast, but still none of them felt the least bit sleepy. The wind moaned outside.

"I've got an idea," said Bertie. "Let's tell *ghost stories*."

"No!" wailed Eugene.

"What's the matter? Scared you might have nightmares?" taunted Darren. "I love ghost stories, the scarier the better."

"Who's going first then?" asked Bertie.

"Eugene," said Darren.

"Why me?" moaned Eugene. "I don't know any ghost stories."

"Just make one up," said Bertie. "And to make it even spookier we'll turn off our torches."

Dirty Bertie

Eugene turned pale. "But it'll be dark."

"Great," said Darren. "I love the dark."

"Me too," said Bertie. "Everyone ready?"

CLICK! Off went the torches. The tent was plunged into blackness.

Eugene cleared his throat. "Once upon a time there were three bears…"

Darren groaned. "That's not a ghost story!"

"It is, it's about ghosts."

"You said it was about three bears!"

"It is. They're ghost bears."

Eugene started again. "Once upon a time there were three ghost bears who lived in a little ghost cottage in the ghost wood…"

"This is rubbish!" grumbled Darren. "It's a fairy story!"

"No it isn't!"

"Yes it is! I bet Goldilocks comes and sits on the ghost chairs and eats the ghost porridge!"

"If you're so clever you tell a story," said Eugene sulkily.

Bertie saw his chance. "I've got one," he said. He was going to tell a story so hair-raising that Darren would be begging him to stop.

"It was a dark, dark night," Bertie began. "The wind was moaning."

"Wooo wooooo!" moaned Darren.

"Three boys were camping in a spooky haunted wood. Suddenly they heard—"

Bertie broke off.

"W-what? Suddenly they heard what?" asked Eugene.

"Shhh!" said Bertie. "Listen!"

"Don't!" whimpered Eugene. "You're scaring me."

"Oooh, me too!" said Darren, giggling.

Bertie shook his head. "I'm serious. I think I heard something."

"It's a ghost! We're all going to DIEEEEE!" wailed Darren, clutching his throat and falling back on his pillow.

"Shut up!" hissed Bertie. "Listen!"

They all held their breath and listened. THUMP!

Help! thought Bertie. *There really is something out there.*

Dirty Bertie

Footsteps came down the path. Closer and closer. Bertie froze. Darren gripped his arm. Suddenly the tent flap was unzipped and they were blinded by light.

"ARGHHHHHHH!" they yelled.

"What's going on?" Mum shone a torch in their faces. "I came to check if everyone was OK."

Bertie heaved a sigh of relief. "We're fine," he said. "We were just going to sleep."

"Yes," said Eugene. "Only first I need the toilet!"

CHAPTER 4

"Eugene?" whispered Bertie. "Eugene, are you awake?"

Eugene snored.

"Darren?"

Darren wheezed. Only Bertie couldn't sleep. How long had he been lying awake? Hours and hours. It must be the middle of the night. The ground was hard, his feet were like blocks of ice and a howling draught was coming from somewhere. Worst of all, he kept thinking he could hear noises outside. Strange, scuffling, moving-about noises.

"Mum?" called Bertie, anxiously. "Mum, is that you?"

No answer. His parents would be fast asleep by now. They wouldn't hear him, even if he screamed. Of course he was only imagining things. It was the wind in the trees. Or the tent creaking. It couldn't be anything else – like a headless ghost for instance. Ghosts were only in ghost stories. If he peeped outside there was no chance at all he'd see a ghost. But just in case, maybe it was safer to stay in the tent. Nothing could get at him in here … unless it came through the walls.

Dirty Bertie

THUD!

Bertie sat bolt upright. He had *definitely* heard something that time. He switched on his torch. How he wished he was back in his own bed. Whose stupid idea was it to sleep outside in a tent? Didn't his parents care if he was eaten alive?

SCUFFLE, SCUFFLE, SCUFFLE.

"HELLO?" croaked Bertie.

No answer. If he was going to come face to face with a headless ghost, he didn't want to do it alone.

"Darren!" he hissed.

Darren went on snoring.

"Darren, wake up!"

"Urhhhh? Whasssgoingon?"

"Listen!" said Bertie. "Something's out there!"

Darren yawned and rolled over. "Yeah, yeah. Nice try, Bertie."

"No, I'm not joking this time! There is!"

Darren raised his head an inch.

SCRATCH, SCRATCH, SCRATCH.

He gasped. He reached under his pillow for his space gun. Bertie gripped his pirate dagger and put a finger to his lips. Maybe if they were quiet as mice the ghost would pass on by?

Dirty Bertie

THUMP!

Arghhh! It was right outside the tent. Bertie could hear its heavy breathing. He froze in horror. The door of the tent was gaping open! Eugene must have forgotten to zip it up when he'd come back from the toilet. No wonder the tent was as cold as the grave!

Bertie pointed. "Close … the … zip!"

"You close it!" squeaked Darren.

The thing was scratching at the tent, trying to get in. Bertie pointed the beam of his torch. Help!

A gigantic shadow with savage teeth and a monstrous head loomed on the side of the tent.

The next moment the thing burst in and was on top of him.

"GET IT OFF! IT'S EATING ME!" screamed Bertie.

"HA! HA! HA!" Darren was doubled up with laughter.

Bertie sat up, pushing the monster off him. He stared at his floppy-eared attacker, who was now crunching on a muesli bar.

"WHIFFER! How did he get out?"

Darren grinned. "Someone must have forgotten to close the back door."

"Eugene!" said Bertie. "I'll kill him. Wait a moment. Where is he?"

They both shone their torches. From the corner of the tent came the sound of peaceful snoring.

Mum unzipped the flap, flooding the tent with morning light.

"Good morning!" she said, brightly. "How did you all sleep?"

"Great, thanks!" Eugene sat up and stretched.

In his sleeping bag, Bertie groaned. All night long he'd had Whiffer lying on top of him, tossing and turning and whining in his sleep. Eugene and Darren

had taken it in turns to snore the
loudest. Bertie hadn't slept a wink.

"Who's for breakfast?" asked Mum.
"Bacon and eggs?"

Bertie turned a shade of green. He
wriggled out of his sleeping bag and
crawled out of the tent.

"Bertie?" said Mum. "Where are you
going?"

"Back to bed!" groaned Bertie.